FOR SNORRI
x

First published 2016 by Two Hoots
an imprint of Pan Macmillan
20 New Wharf Road, London N1 9RR
Associated companies throughout the world
www.panmacmillan.com
ISBN: 978-1-5098-0894-6
Text and illustrations © Morag Hood 2016
Moral rights asserted.

1 3 5 7 9 8 6 4 2
A CIP catalogue record for this book is available from the British Library.
Printed in China
The illustrations in this book were created using supermarket carrier bags.

www.twohootsbooks.com

MORAG HOOD

Colin and Lee
Carrot and Pea

TWO HOOTS

This is Lee.

He is a pea.

All of his friends are peas.

Except Colin.

Colin isn't a pea.

He is much too tall
to be a pea,

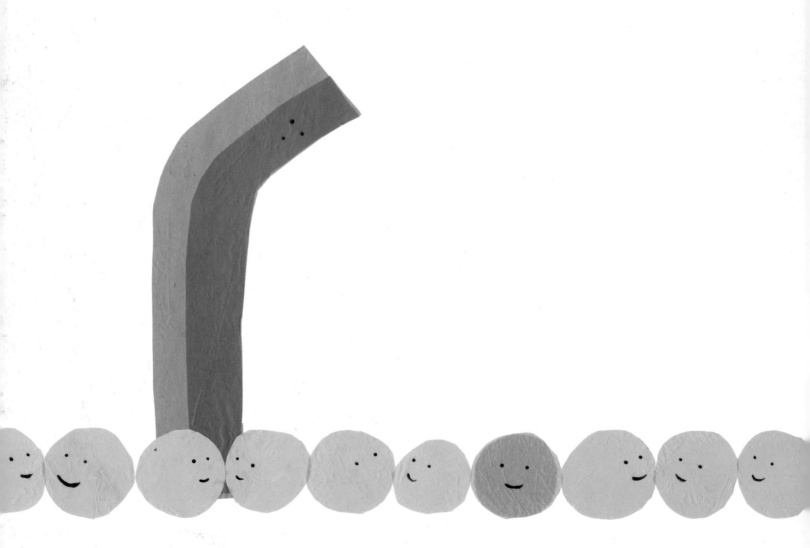

and very orange.

He can't roll like a pea,

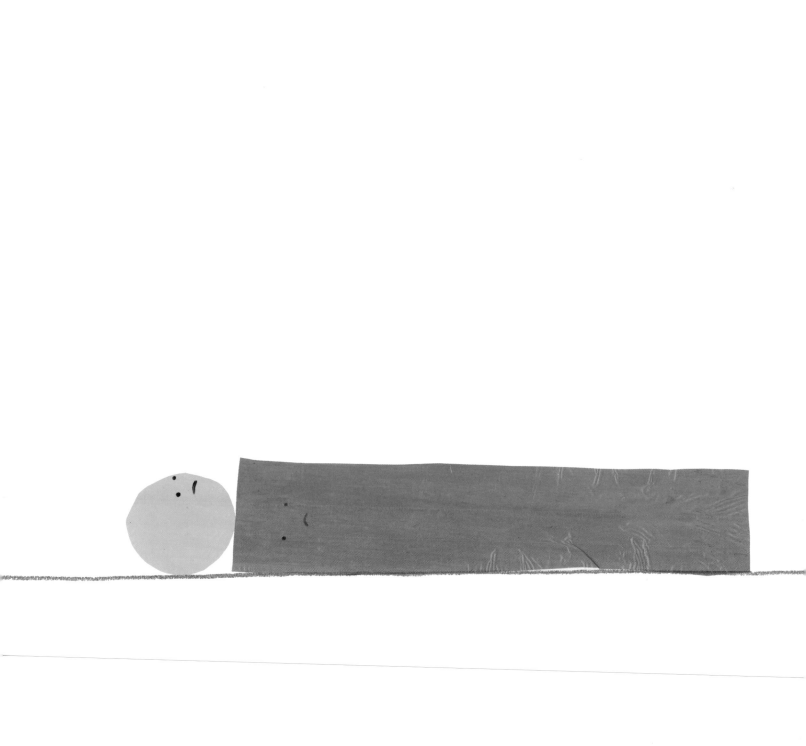

or bounce like a pea.

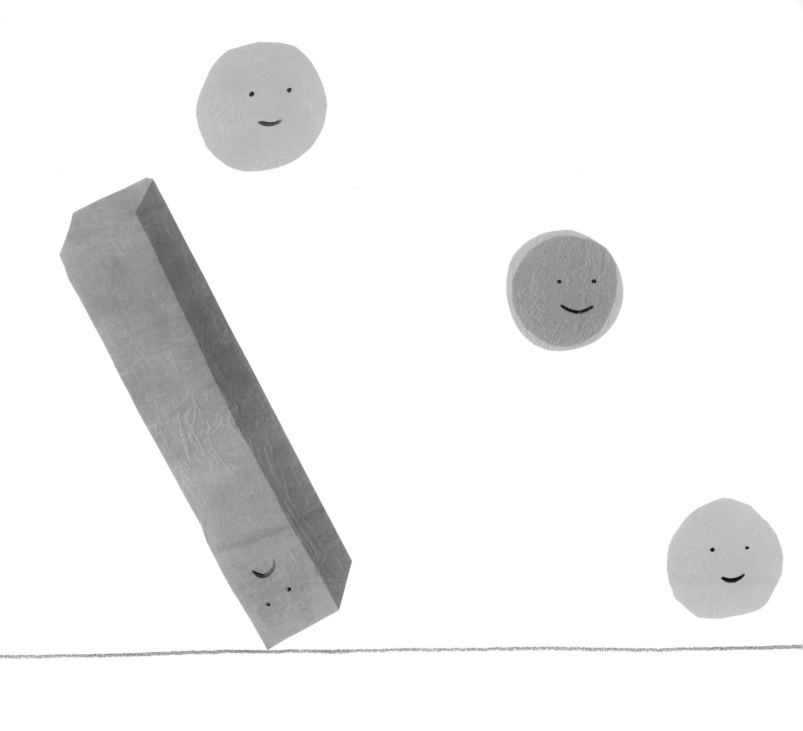

And he isn't very good at
playing hide-and-seek.

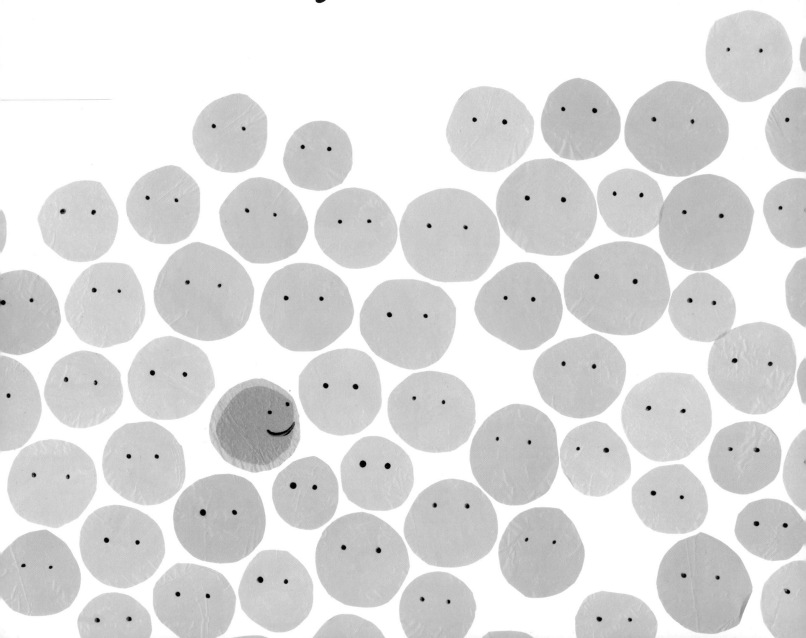

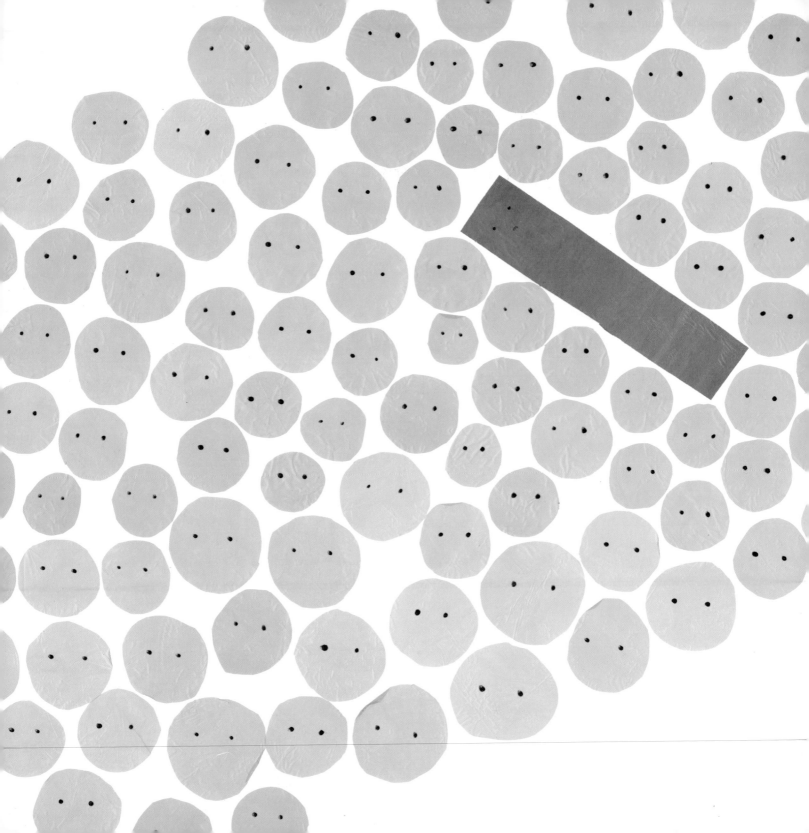

But Colin makes an
excellent tower,

a fantastic bridge,

and a great slide.

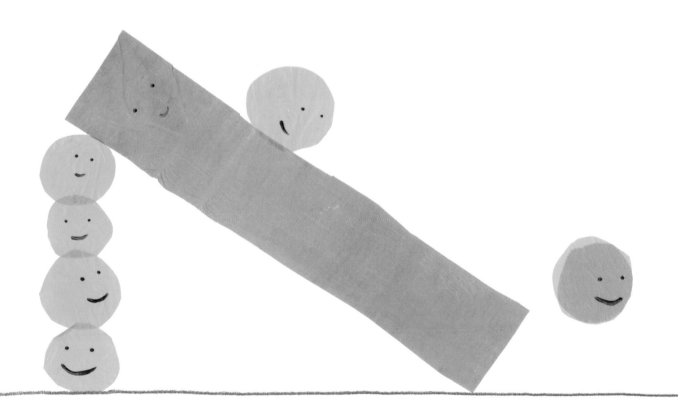

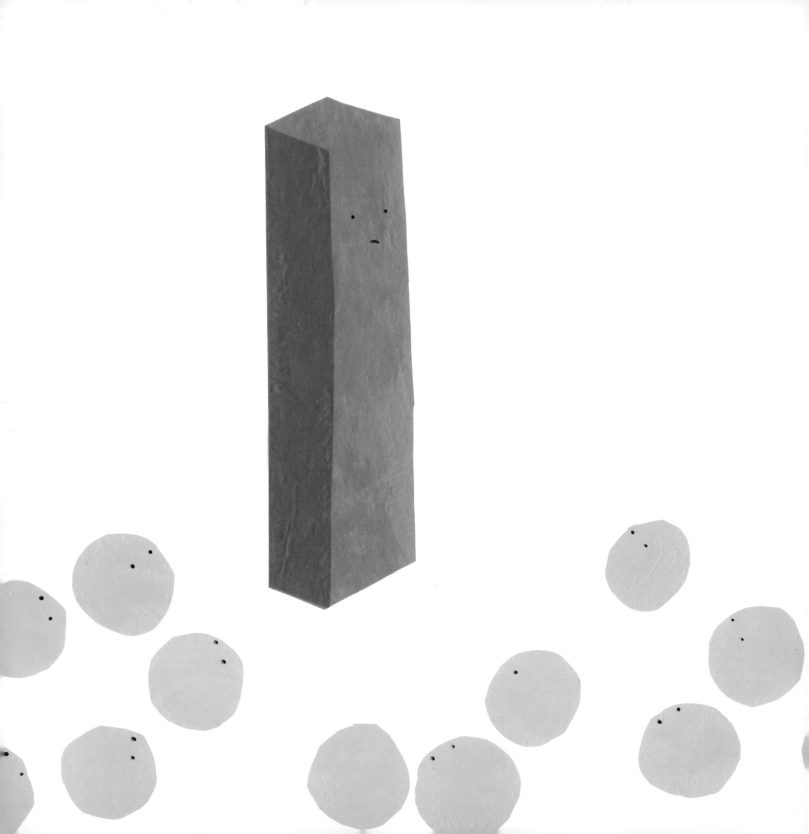

Colin isn't at all like Lee
and the other peas,

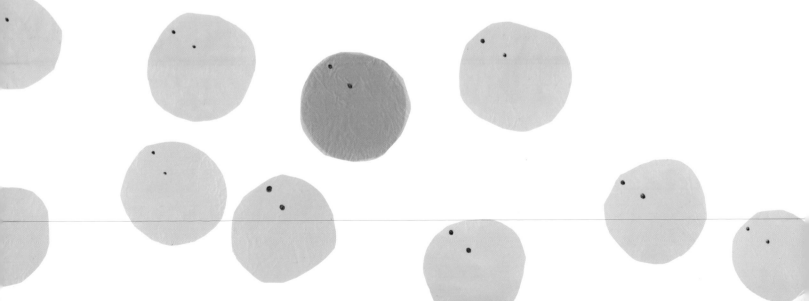

but they are

the best of friends.